DID YOU GET THE CAT?

B.I. PHILLIPS

To order additional copies of this book, contact:
Xlibris
844-714-8691
www.Xlibris.com
Orders@Xlibris.com

ISBN: Softcover   978-1-6698-5776-1
         EBook   978-1-6698-5775-4

Print information available on the last page

Rev. date: 11/29/2022

Grateful acknowledgements to: Blue Pearl, Humane Society of Tampa Bay, Pet Resource Center, The Marriott at Citrus Park, Lake Cane Tennis Center, Winter Park Tennis Center, Fort King Tennis Center and HCC tennis.

This book belongs to:

_____

One day while driving home from a tennis match at HCC Tennis complex ahead on the road I couldn't believe I saw small grey kitten heading out into a three lane highway.

Instinctively I pulled off the road ran out into the three lanes like I was fully trained to do this type of thing which I wasn't.

Put up my hand as a warning.

Grabbed the small grey kitten and wrapped a towel around him/ her and proceeded to the nearest animal hospital.

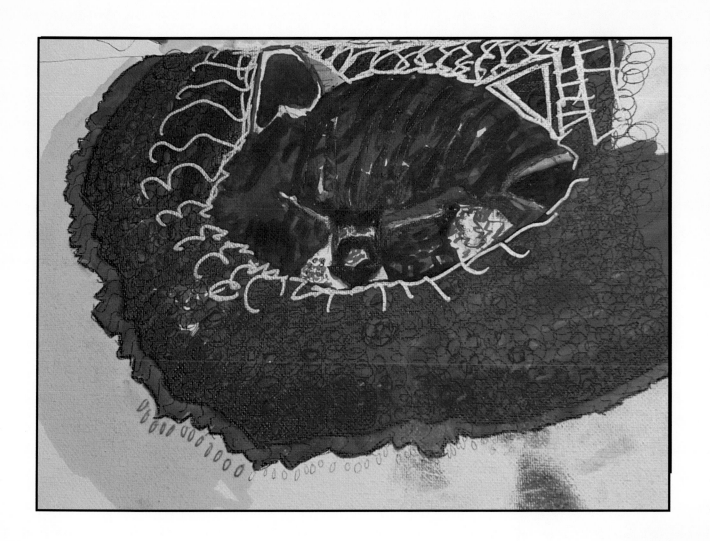

The poor kitten lost control of his excretory system which I saw as a negative sign and I prayed fervently that God would please let this little kitten survive.

Well when I arrived they took the kitten right away and came out saying he/ she would be okay and did I want this kitten?

Remembering the wise words from my on again off again husband Peter I thought I already have two and leave it for someone who needs one.

Lo and behold my art teacher was very insistent that I get this cat. So the journey began to find this cat. Jan 2018.

In between the hours of looking for the cat came Heidi the Australian Shepherd. Heidi scared herself the first time she passed gas and jumped and looked behind her.

The next day I went to the Social Science building at USF. I found out they were training dogs to sniff out stolen artifacts. I wondered how they did this so I began to investigate. I found out they lift the fingerprints off the artifact to give the dog the scent.

After this I went back to Blue Pearl to find out where this kitten went. They said check animal services. They also said the kitten may have been returned to where it was found. I thought how stupid so the kitten would run back out into the road again. Feb 2018.

So off I went to animal services. Arriving there I did not see the kitten.

Off to the Humane Society I went. They said did the cat have a microchip number.

Off I went to Blue Pearl to see if the cat had gotten a microchip in which I was told they were not sure. August 2019.

For weeks I went back and forth from animal services to the Humane Society. Dec. 2018.

Christina's 2019 came and went. My Christmas tree was a painting I had painted of a Christmas tree with ornaments.

New Year's Eve 2019 came and went.

Then one day I went to the Humane Society and saw what I thought was my former art teachers cat and then I realized how CRUEL life really is. March 2020.

I tried to adopt the cat we believed belonged to our former art teacher but was told this cat would not do well in a home with other cats.

I asked a friend who had no cats to adopt this cat. July 2020.

In November of 2020 after being rear ended by an off duty UPS driver(illustration) I tested positive for Covid. I was housebound for two weeks and couldn't look for the cat.

Christmas 2020 came and went. Peter bought a Christmas tree that didn't work so he took it back and didn't get another one which I thought was weird. I love told my archeologist friend Alan about this.

New Year's Eve came and went. 2020.

Remembering the cat I mistook for our art teachers cat that I got a good vibe from I thought I will go and visit this cat. So I did for weeks and week. I bought the cat a toy. Tested the cat for play desire. The cat did not really seem interested in the toy but made a few feeble attempts at play.

Then one day the cat was no longer there. Sad but happy for this cat I thought I will see if this cat comes back.

Daily I looked at the websites because I knew it was important to my teacher that I find this grey cat from the highway. Saw a few possibilities but when arrived to look at the cat either the age or adoption data didn't match.

Christmas 2021 came and went. This Christmas I stayed out at the Citrus Park Marriott. They had a beautiful Christmas Tree and finally two years I was able to have a Christmas tree even if it wasn't my own.

Later that month in January I played in a tennis tournament in Orlando. I brought my hamster Chip. On the way home we stopped at a rest area. I let him out to walk a little bit. Highly supervised of course. I couldn't believe when he started climbing a tree.

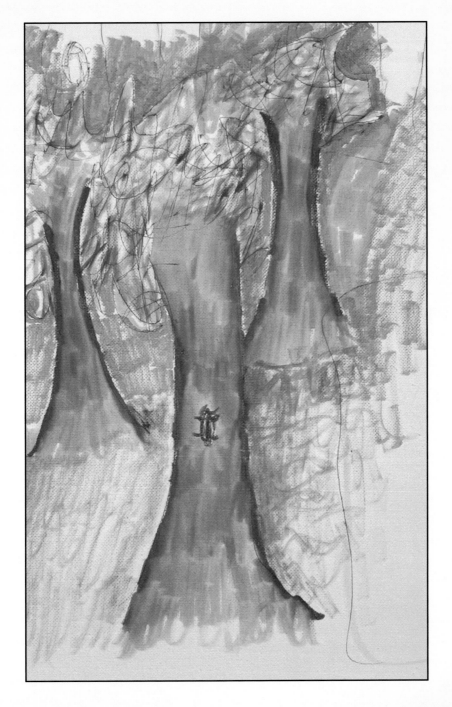

While there I met a family who had been camping at a local KOA. They said they had never seen anyone walk a hamster before.

When arriving back from yet another trip looking for this cat I noticed a loud humming noise and I looked at the Jasmine tree and I noticed a flurry of bees in the tree. I ran to ask what is going on. Peter said they are feeding from the tree. I took a video. I couldn't believe it. When I came back the tree was almost bare. Flower blossoms all over the ground.

Later that day I thought I would assimilate myself to be like Peter and feed the ducks. I bought bread and went to where the ducks are. I couldn't believe my luck. While I was there the biggest most beautiful birds flew in.

Then something horrible happened. A fish tried to eat the bread that fell in the water and a bird tried to eat the fish. I thought I will not do this again. Sept 2022.

Back to the humane society website I noticed the grey cat that resembled our art teachers cat had come back. Another art classmate assured me that this cat was not our art teacher Gainors cat. So back to looking for the small grey kitten from the highway. September 2022.

I wondered if I would have a Christmas tree for 2022.

Then came Hurricane IAN.

After remembering the good vibe I felt from this old 12 year old cat that resembled our art teachers cat that I couldn't have I began collecting pictures of cats that resembled this cat.

After 5 years of looking for this cat I began to pray that if God wanted me to find this cat that he would have to intercede.

Frequently I go to the Riveria restaurant for breakfast. This day as I was walking in I saw an abject at the last minute. When I realized it was a bullfrog I screamed and jumped. I wasn't sure if it was alive or not. (illustrations)went inside and Kathy told me workers had smashed him with a shovel. Instantly I started thinking poor bullfrog. Stupid and ignorant people.

46

Upon leaving the restaurant I noticed a woman in the large industrial dumpster. I said hi and thought how cool.

Later that week I brought Chip the hamster to visit his uncle Jason. Nearby were several storage units. Before I knew it Chip the hamster took off and ran under the door of one of the storage units. Number 9 of all the units. After the fire department told me it's a myth that they get cats out of trees God put a stranger in my path that led me to the person with the key to the lock on storage unit number 9. Finally with Uncle Jason's help we got Chip the hamster out of storage unit number 9.

Next we have Hurricane Nicole. I found out which shelters allow pets. Then am told they must have anti- rabies credentials. Well trying to catch these cats is not easy.

In thinking about the year of so many tennis tournaments I think about the many new friends I have made and so many rules I have learned either through being accused of breaking them or seeing them broken in others. For example, escalating a point, delaying a point and non compliant medical time- outs. In which I had to take 2. One in Ocala and one in Kissimmee.

All in all I am still looking for the cat and wondering what this Christmas 2022 will hold.

Printed in the United States
by Baker & Taylor Publisher Services